SHARON GARLOUGH BROWN

Feathers of Hope

Study Guide

EIGHT WEEKS FOR INDIVIDUALS OR GROUPS

An imprint of InterVarsity Press
Downers Grove, Illinois

InterVarsity Press
P.O. Box 1400, Downers Grove, IL 60515-1426
ivpress.com
email@ivpress.com

*InterVarsity Press® is the book-publishing division of InterVarsity Christian Fellowship/USA®, a movement of
students and faculty active on campus at hundreds of universities, colleges, and schools of nursing in the United
States of America, and a member movement of the International Fellowship of Evangelical Students. For
information about local and regional activities, visit intervarsity.org.*

*Scripture quotations, unless otherwise noted, are from the New Revised Standard Version Bible, copyright © 1989
National Council of the Churches of Christ in the United States of America. Used by permission. All rights
reserved worldwide.*

*This is a work of fiction. People, places, events, and situations are either the product of the author's imagination or
are used fictitiously. Any resemblance to events, locales, or actual persons, living or dead, is entirely coincidental.*

*The publisher cannot verify the accuracy or functionality of website URLs used in this book beyond the date of
publication.*

Cover design and image composite: David Fassett
Interior design: Daniel van Loon
Images: abstract floral background: © andipantz / iStock / Getty Images Plus
    textured gradient cloudscape: © DavidMSchrader / iStock / Getty Images Plus
    sunflower: © Francesco Carta fotografo / Moment / Getty Images
    black ink rolled out: © IntergalacticDesignStudio / E+ / Getty Images
    red Cardinal bird: © Jeff R Clow / Moment / Getty Images
    abstract watercolor painting: © philsajonesen / E+ / Getty Images
    designed acrylic background: © Wylius / iStock / Getty Images Plus
    light blue painted texture: ©andipantz / iStock / Getty Images Plus

ISBN 978-1-5140-0064-9 (print)
ISBN 978-1-5140-0065-6 (digital)

P   25   24   23   22   21   20   19   18   17   16   15   14   13   12   11   10   9   8   7   6   5   4   3   2

Y   43   42   41   40   39   38   37   36   35   34   33   32   31   30   29   28   27   26   25   24   23   22

CONTENTS

INTRODUCTION

F*eathers of Hope* is a book that invites reflection, not only on the retreat content Katherine Rhodes offers but on the journeys the characters make as they seek to respond faithfully to God's love and grace. Though this study guide is formatted to be completed in eight weeks, I hope you'll take this journey at an unhurried pace, giving yourself ample time to process, pray, and respond to whatever the Holy Spirit reveals to you.

Each week contains five days of Scripture readings and reflection questions, with a sixth day for review. You're also invited each week to pray with a painting or sketch by Vincent van Gogh (search online for the listed title, date, and museum location). You can decide whether to read *Feathers of Hope* first in its entirety and then return to do a slow study with the guide, or to read it a section at a time as you explore the daily questions. Some chapters have multiple days.

I recommend keeping a travelogue of your journey. Even if you aren't in the habit of using a journal, you'll benefit from having a record of what you're noticing as you move forward. Not every question will resonate with you. That's okay. You don't need to answer every question every day. But do watch for any impulse to avoid a question because it agitates you or makes you feel uncomfortable. Perhaps that's the most important one for you to ponder. You may also find that the characters' journeys tap deep things for you that aren't addressed in the questions. I encourage you to stay with what stirs you as you reflect and pray.

Some questions and themes are repeated as you journey with the guide, and you may be tempted to say, "I already answered that." Listen with fresh ears. Is anything new emerging? Shifting? Coming into sharper focus? Use the questions as launching points for your journaling.

Included in the guide are group discussion questions. Though I long for every reader to have the opportunity to share the journey with even one trustworthy traveling companion, I know community can be a challenge both to find and practice well. I encourage you to be brave and invite others to join you in this study.

As you travel with this guide, I hope the characters will become windows and mirrors for seeing yourself and God more clearly. May the Lord direct your steps and give you courage. And may he enlarge your capacity to receive his love, comfort, and grace so you can offer these generous gifts to others.

Peace to you,

Sharon Garlough Brown

May the God of hope fill you with all joy and
peace as you trust in him, so that you may overflow
with hope by the power of the Holy Spirit.

Romans 15:13 (NIV)

WEEK ONE

Chapters One Through Four

⋏⋏➤

VISIO DIVINA: *WORN OUT* (1882, PENCIL ON PAPER,
VAN GOGH MUSEUM, AMSTERDAM)

Visio divina ("sacred seeing") is similar in practice to *lectio divina* ("sacred reading"). In *lectio divina* we are invited into a slow and prayerful pondering of Scripture, paying attention to the words or phrases that stir us and lead us into conversation and communion with God. In *visio divina* we are invited into a slow and prayerful pondering of visual images (paintings, photographs, sculpture, etc.), noticing the details that catch our attention and draw us into conversation and communion with God.

Each week, you can choose when and how often to pray with the art. To begin, find an online image of the work. Then ask God to guide your attention as you look at it. If you are new to the practice of praying with art, you might find the provided reflection prompts helpful.

The weary and bent elderly man, Adrianus Jacobus Zuyderland, lived at the Dutch Reformed Almshouse for Men and Women in The Hague. Vincent made several drawings of *Worn Out* before creating a lithograph of the work. He later changed the title of the lithograph to *At Eternity's Gate.* (If you're interested in reading how Vincent interpreted this image, visit www.vangoghletters.org and search for letter #288, November 1882.)

Begin by quieting yourself in God's presence. Then let your gaze rove slowly over the sketch. What words come to mind to describe the mood of the drawing? What memories or feelings are evoked in you as you look at him? Which part of the drawing most captures your attention and invites you to linger? Why? How does this sketch mirror your own life or the lives of those you love?

Speak with God about what is stirred in you as you "read" the painting in prayer. What do you need from God right now?

WEEK ONE: DAY ONE   *Chapter One*

Scripture Contemplation: 2 Corinthians 5:1-4

> For we know that if the earthly tent we live in is destroyed, we have a building from God, a house not made with hands, eternal in the heavens. For in this tent we groan, longing to be clothed with our heavenly dwelling—if indeed, when we have taken it off we will not be found naked. For while we are still in this tent, we groan under our burden, because we wish not to be unclothed but to be further clothed, so that what is mortal may be swallowed up by life.

Read the verses aloud. Which images or promises connect with your life or longings right now? Speak with God about whatever stirs you.

FOR REFLECTION

1. What does this opening chapter reveal about who Wren is? Which of her traits, gifts, or struggles stand out to you? Why?

2. The image of the molting cardinal catches Wren's attention, both for her own life and for the people she serves. Think about your own experiences of gradual or dramatic loss and change. How does this image speak to you?

3. What would you put in your shadow box? What do these items declare about your passions, history, loved ones, or losses? (If you are participating in a group study, choose an item to bring with you to your meeting.)

4. What evidence of molting do you see in others' lives? In your local community? In the world? How are you being prompted to pray? Offer your response to God.

WEEK ONE: DAY TWO   *Chapter Two*

Scripture Contemplation: Matthew 11:28-30

Come to me, all you that are weary and are carrying heavy burdens, and I will give you rest. Take my yoke upon you, and learn from me; for I am gentle and humble in heart, and you will find rest for your souls. For my yoke is easy, and my burden is light.

Quiet yourself in God's presence with a few deep breaths. When you're ready, open your hands and release to Jesus any weariness or burdens that weigh you down. Keeping your hands open, receive from him the gifts he longs to pour out to you. Throughout the day, open your hands to release burdens and receive Jesus' rest.

FOR REFLECTION

1. What evidence of molting do you glimpse in Kit's life? In what ways do you identify with her?

2. What would you place in a file marked "transition"? Consider personal, cultural, and global upheaval and change. Which kinds of transitions are hardest for you to embrace? Why? Speak with God about what you notice.

3. Look at Vincent's *Worn Out* sketch. Would you be more like Mara, ready to kiss and encourage the weary man, or like Kit, ready to sit alongside and share the silence with him? What do you need from others when you're exhausted or despairing?

4. How confident are you in God's love for you? For others? Is it easier to share God's love with others or receive it for yourself? Why? Speak with God about any longings or resistance.

WEEK ONE: DAY THREE   *Chapter Two*

Scripture Contemplation: Isaiah 42:1-4

Here is my servant, whom I uphold,
    my chosen, in whom my soul delights;
I have put my spirit upon him;
    he will bring forth justice to the nations.
He will not cry or lift up his voice,
    or make it heard in the street;
a bruised reed he will not break,
    and a dimly burning wick he will not quench;
    he will faithfully bring forth justice.
He will not grow faint or be crushed

until he has established justice in the earth;
and the coastlands wait for his teaching.

Slowly read the verses aloud. Which descriptions of the Messiah speak most deeply to you? Why? Speak with God about what you notice.

FOR REFLECTION

1. What kinds of needs or issues are you most passionate about? Why? How have your personal struggles, losses, and hopes shaped your engagement with others, individually and in society?

2. How does Kit respond to Mara's stories about conflict and her efforts to address racial bias at Crossroads? Does her internal reaction resonate with you? Frustrate you? Why? Talk honestly with God about your reaction to this scene.

3. What does the word *justice* evoke for you? Is there any resistance or fear attached to the word? If so, why?

4. Is it easy for you to care about issues and needs that don't directly impact you or your loved ones? Why or why not? Speak with God about what you notice.

5. In what ways does the image of pinfeathers speak to you?

WEEK ONE: DAY FOUR *Chapter Three*

Scripture Contemplation: 1 Corinthians 13:4-7

Love is patient; love is kind; love is not envious or boastful or arrogant or rude. It does not insist on its own way; it is not irritable or resentful; it does not rejoice in wrongdoing, but rejoices in the truth. It bears all things, believes all things, hopes all things, endures all things.

Slowly and prayerfully read the verses aloud. Then meditate on each description of love, considering how God has loved you in these ways. Take time to receive this kind of generous love from God. Notice any resistance, either to a description of love or to your receiving it. Which descriptions most challenge or comfort you? Why?

FOR REFLECTION

1. Which elements of Wren's grief or forgiveness process resonate with you? Speak with God about what you see.

2. Ponder Wren's imagined triptych of cardinals: life before molting, life during molting, life after molting. What helps you practice hope during seasons of loss and change? In what ways has suffering marked you?

3. Which words or themes usually come to mind when you think about stewardship? Which of the retreat themes Kit has planned (stewarding love, stewarding affliction, stewarding grace) most intrigues you? Why?

4. What does it look like to practice "long-suffering" love in a culture that is quick to anger and prone to disregard or "cancel" others? How might the regular and habitual practice of receiving God's love enlarge and enable you to love those who aren't easy to love? Speak with God about what you need.

5. What catches your attention from Kit's prayerful pondering of Vincent's *The Sower*? (You'll have an opportunity next week to pray with this painting.) What is the sower's call or invitation to you? How will you respond?

WEEK ONE: DAY FIVE   *Chapter Four*

Scripture Contemplation: 1 Corinthians 13:4-7

Love is patient; love is kind; love is not envious or boastful or arrogant or rude. It does not insist on its own way; it is not irritable or resentful; it does not rejoice in wrongdoing, but rejoices in the truth. It bears all things, believes all things, hopes all things, endures all things.

Slowly and prayerfully read the verses aloud. As you read, picture the people (or types of people) you find most difficult to love, the ones who don't have "easy access" to your affection. Which qualities of love are hardest for you to offer others? Speak honestly to God about what you see and what you need.

FOR REFLECTION

1. What is your initial impression of Sarah? Is she someone you would find easy to love? Why or why not?

2. Identify some of the issues Sarah and Kit disagree about. How do you navigate conflict and disagreement with others? How does Kit's reminder of the fractured state of the church at Corinth influence the way you read and receive Paul's words about love?

3. "What we ourselves have generously and abundantly received, we freely offer to others." Why is it essential to focus on how God has loved us as we try to love others well? How is this connected with the practice of stewardship?

4. Ponder these words from Kit: "When you recognize a lack of love in your own heart, name it to God and receive God's grace and forgiveness and power. Remember, this isn't an exercise in self-condemnation but an opportunity to diligently seek God for a gift he longs to give you in greater and greater measure." Read 1 Corinthians 13:4-7 again. What do you need from God as you seek to love not in generalities, but in specifics?

WEEK ONE: DAY SIX *Review*

Return to any reflection questions you weren't able to respond to this week. Prayerfully review your notes. Do any particular themes, struggles, longings, or invitations emerge for you? Speak with God about what you notice. (If you'd like to do an extended prayer exercise with John 13 and the story of Jesus washing the disciples' feet, see my book *Barefoot.*)

WEEK ONE

Group Discussion

One of the best gifts we can give one another in community is the promise of confidentiality. As you begin to walk together, commit to creating a safe place. Devote yourselves to being faithful stewards of one another's stories. Only then are we truly free to offer our authentic selves to one another, without fear of being judged or betrayed. As you continue to journey together, remind yourselves frequently of your commitment to each other. Pray for God to guard, protect, and establish you in your life together.

When you gather, avoid the impulse to give advice, "fix," or commiserate ("I know just how you feel because something similar happened to me when . . ."). Give space to pregnant silence. Don't rush to fill the quiet, even if it feels uncomfortable or awkward. Trust that the Holy Spirit is stirring hearts in the midst of the silence and giving courage to speak. (This will be a particularly important gift to offer the introverts in your group.) Practice listening for the presence of God in both the silence and the words offered. Encourage one another to share from the heart, without compelling anyone to do so. Gently and lovingly remind one another to return to these practices of life together whenever you find yourself drifting off course.

Each week you'll find suggested group questions, but feel free to modify these according to the needs and desires of your group. As you find your rhythm together, you may simply want to share in an open-ended way what God is stirring as a result of your prayerful reflections during the week. Resist the temptation to be distracted by "book club" discussions. Instead, let the characters' journeys lead you into fruitful, honest conversations about how God is shaping and forming you as you reflect and pray.

Some of the issues raised in *Feathers of Hope* are emotionally charged and difficult to talk about. They may also tap deep wounds. Give one another (and yourself) lots of grace as you navigate these topics and themes. Go gently. Walk humbly. And ask for the courage to listen well as you practice loving one another.

It's a gift to share the journey with others. May your group time be sacred space in the presence of God.

(Group leaders: Each week, choose one of the Scripture texts from the daily readings as an opening prayer. If possible, light a Christ candle to remind yourselves that you are in the presence of God together. You may also wish to have a digital or printed image of the *visio divina* piece available for prayer or discussion.)

Intro: If your group hasn't met before, offer introductions and share one personal desire as you begin the study. What do you hope you'll be able to say at the end of the journey in eight weeks?

1. As a way of continuing your introductions to one another, share (or describe) an item you would put into a shadow box. What does this item reveal about who you are and what you value?

2. Discuss the image of molting. How does it speak to you? What evidence of molting do you see in your own life? Your community? The world? (Let these reflections shape your time of prayer at the end of your meeting.)

3. What are some of the issues you're most passionate about? Why? If you're comfortable, share something that Kit and Mara's conversation prompted you to ponder or remember about your own engagement with (or avoidance of) issues of race and justice.

4. Share any aha moments from the first retreat session about stewarding love. What do you need from God? How can the group pray for you?

5. Any other insights to share from the week? What challenged or inspired you? Why? Close by reading 1 Corinthians 13:4-7 in unison and pray for one another.

WEEK TWO
Chapters Five Through Twelve

VISIO DIVINA: *THE SOWER* (NOVEMBER 1888, VAN GOGH MUSEUM, AMSTERDAM)

During his career Vincent made more than thirty drawings and paintings of sowers, many of them adaptations of Jean-François Millet's work. This one, however, is original to him. In a letter to his brother, Theo, Vincent included a sketch of it and told him which colors he was using (Letter #722, November 1888).

Quiet yourself in God's presence. Then let your gaze wander slowly over the painting, noticing colors and composition. What thoughts or feelings emerge as you look at the painting? Which details catch your attention and cause you to linger? How do these details connect with your life or longings? Talk with God about what you notice. What is God's invitation to you?

(For further prayer this week, you might ponder Jesus' sower parables in Mark 4:1-20 and Mark 4:26-29.)

WEEK TWO: DAY ONE   *Chapters Five and Six*

Scripture Contemplation: Romans 12:9-12

> Let love be genuine; hate what is evil, hold fast to what is good; love one another with mutual affection; outdo one another in showing honor. Do not lag in zeal, be ardent in spirit, serve the Lord. Rejoice in hope, be patient in suffering, persevere in prayer.

Slowly read the verses aloud, letting them lead you into prayer. Where do you see evidence of the Spirit's fruit and work in your life? What do you need from God? Make the petitions personal: "Let my love be genuine; may I hate what is evil and hold fast to what is good," and so on.

Now recast the Scripture passage into a petition for all God's people: "Lord, let our love be genuine. May we hate what is evil and hold fast to what is good; may we love one another with mutual affection; may we outdo one another in showing honor. Let us not lag in zeal. May we be ardent in spirit. May we serve you. Help us rejoice in hope, be patient in suffering, and persevere in prayer."

FOR REFLECTION

1. What hobbies or creative pursuits give you joy? Are they part of your regular rhythm of life? If not, how might you incorporate them into your rhythm?

2. What does the interaction with Mrs. Whitlock's daughter trigger for Wren? How do you typically respond when you're accused?

3. What relational dynamics catch your attention in these chapters? Do any of them mirror your own history, habits, or struggles? Offer God what you notice.

4. Sarah wonders, "Why not speak encouragement and affirmation and thanks to the living? Why not celebrate a life well-lived while that person still lived?" Who might God be calling

you to encourage, thank, or honor? What could you offer as a gift of affirmation?

WEEK TWO: DAY TWO   *Chapters Seven and Eight*

Scripture Contemplation: Romans 14:10-12

Why do you pass judgment on your brother or sister? Or you, why do you despise your brother or sister? For we will all stand before the judgment seat of God. For it is written,
> "As I live, says the Lord, every knee shall bow to me,
> and every tongue shall give praise to God."
So then, each of us will be accountable to God.

Read the verses slowly, listening as the Spirit addresses you. How do you respond to the questions? To the declarations? Bring your honest responses into conversation with God.

FOR REFLECTION

1. What do you notice about Kit's reaction to news and details about the candidate? Does anything surprise you? Resonate with you? Why?

2. How quickly do you tend to rush to judgment about people you don't know? Is there anyone you need to practice offering the benefit of the doubt to? Speak with God about what you see.

3. As Wren is feeling accused and rejected, she remembers her painting of Jesus (available to view in my book *Remember Me*) and

ponders his solidarity with her. How does Jesus' experience of being despised, condemned, and rejected speak to you? In what ways have you experienced his solidarity and faithfulness, or how do you long to? Have a conversation with him about this.

4. If you were to paint your emotions today, what colors would you use? Why?

5. How do you process the kind of change you do not choose and do not want? Which examples of this kind of change can you name in your life? How has God met you in the midst of up-heaval? What do you need from God today?

WEEK TWO: DAY THREE   *Chapters Nine and Ten*

Scripture Contemplation: 2 Corinthians 1:3-4

Blessed be the God and Father of our Lord Jesus Christ, the Father of mercies and the God of all consolation, who consoles us in all our affliction, so that we may be able to console those who are in any affliction with the consolation with which we ourselves are consoled by God.

Read the text slowly and prayerfully. Name to God any current need for consolation in affliction. Recall, too, occasions when God has consoled you in the past. What opportunities have you had for comforting others with the comfort you've received? What opportunities do you have now?

FOR REFLECTION

1. Which details from Wren and Kit's conversations catch your attention, both in what they share and in what they conceal? How freely do you name your own disappointments, sorrows, or struggles to others? How freely do you name them to God? Talk with God about what you see.

2. While Kit is trying to remain fully present to the people and work in front of her, Wren is trying to navigate the juxtaposition of life and death at Willow Springs. Do either of them model anything for you? If so, what?

3. Is the reminder of death a terror or a gift of grace to you? What kind of death would you prefer for yourself? Your loved ones? Why?

4. How does the image of molting continue to speak to Wren? How does it speak to you?

WEEK TWO: DAY FOUR   *Chapter Eleven*

Scripture Contemplation: Psalm 143:1-8

Hear my prayer, O LORD;
    give ear to my supplications in your faithfulness;
    answer me in your righteousness.
Do not enter into judgment with your servant,

for no one living is righteous before you.
For the enemy has pursued me,
    crushing my life to the ground,
    making me sit in darkness like those long dead.
Therefore my spirit faints within me;
    my heart within me is appalled.
I remember the days of old,
    I think about all your deeds,
    I meditate on the works of your hands.
I stretch out my hands to you;
    my soul thirsts for you like a parched land. *Selah*
Answer me quickly, O LORD;
    my spirit fails.
Do not hide your face from me,
    or I shall be like those who go down to the Pit.
Let me hear of your steadfast love in the morning,
    for in you I put my trust.
Teach me the way I should go,
    for to you I lift up my soul.

Read the Scripture passage aloud a few times. Which words catch your attention and stir your longings? Bring what you notice into conversation with God.

FOR REFLECTION

1. Do you tend to pray spontaneously or use written prayers? Do any of Kit's thoughts about the blessing of Ezra's collection of prayers resonate with you? If you haven't used liturgy before, how might set prayers be a gift to you?

2. When do you most need to hear of God's steadfast love? What helps you trust God's steadfast love for yourself? For others? As an embodied prayer, tuck your chin to your shoulder and

picture yourself leaning against Jesus' breast like the beloved disciple. Let your vision widen to include room for the whole weary world to be gathered and held in God's love.

3. In addition to praying with Scripture, Kit prays with art, a holding cross, open hands, her breath, a prayer book, a Christ candle. Which objects or embodied practices help you focus on the presence of God?

4. Choose a printed prayer from this chapter and pray it aloud.

WEEK TWO: DAY FIVE   *Chapter Twelve*

Scripture Contemplation: Numbers 6:24-26

> The LORD bless you and keep you;
> the LORD make his face to shine upon you, and be gracious to you;
> the LORD lift up his countenance upon you, and give you peace.

Pray this blessing for yourself and your loved ones, taking the words to heart. Then widen the blessing out to your larger community, including those who don't have easy access to your affection. Picture their faces and insert their names as you ask God to bless them. Offer to God any resistance to praying this way and ask for his help to speak the words aloud. How might regularly speaking God's blessing upon others shape you?

FOR REFLECTION

1. Have you (like Kit) had people in your life who have spoken truth to you with a fierce and protective love? How have you

received them? How have they demonstrated that they are "for you" even if they wound you?

2. Who do you desire to be free and whole? How has this desire impacted your relationship? Your prayers? The way you offer encouragement or exhortation? Speak with God about what you see.

3. Sarah is trying to discern the best expression of love for her mom. What helps you discern what love looks like?

4. What places, people, or practices help you detach from the demands of *chronos* (chronological time) and yield to the invitations of *kairos* (opportune moments)? How might you practice yielding today?

5. What is your next yes? Have a conversation with God about it.

WEEK TWO: DAY SIX   *Review*

Return to any questions you were unable to answer. Prayerfully review your notes. Do you notice any themes emerging in your life with God and others? Speak with him about what you see.

WEEK TWO

Group Discussion

Group leaders, choose a Scripture text to read as you center yourselves in God's presence. You might also select, adapt, or develop a responsive liturgy for the beginning or end of your meeting. As a final prayer, recite in unison the collective prayer based on Romans 12:9-12, day one.

1. What places, people, or practices help you detach from the demands of *chronos* and yield to the invitations of *kairos*? Were you able to say yes to any of these invitations this week? If so, share an example.

2. Identify some of the relational dynamics you've witnessed between the characters. How do you discern the best expression of love in your own relationships? What challenges do you face in loving well?

3. Discuss some of the struggles the characters are experiencing. In what ways do you identify with them? Do any of them model something for you? If so, what?

4. Which Scripture passages caught your attention this week and drew you into deeper insight and prayer?

5. Which objects or embodied practices help you pray? What have you noticed as you've prayed with art the past couple of weeks? How can the group pray for you?

6. As you prepare to pray together, speak Ezra's written prayer in unison: "May our prayers rise as fragrant incense before you, O Lord. Gather into your heavenly bowls our joys and sorrows, our praise and petitions, our gratitude and our longings for your kingdom to come."

WEEK THREE

Chapters Thirteen Through Fifteen

★ ★ ➤

VISIO DIVINA: *SUNFLOWERS* (AUGUST 1888, NEUE PINAKOTHEK, MUNICH)

Vincent painted eleven different versions of cut sunflowers, some of them in vases and some lying flat. A few of them he painted to welcome fellow artist Paul Gauguin to the Yellow House, where he hoped to form an artists' community. In a letter to Theo, Vincent wrote, "You may know that the peony is Jeannin's, the hollyhock belongs to Quost, but the sunflower is mine in a way" (Letter #741, January 1889).

Take a slow and prayerful look at the painting. What thoughts or emotions are stirred in you as you view it? Which details catch your attention? Why? Speak with God about what you see.

You might also try receiving it as an image for *memento mori:* "Remember you must die." How does reading the painting in this way impact you? Offer God whatever is stirred in you as you ponder your mortality. Is this a morbid or hopeful exercise for you? Why?

WEEK THREE: DAY ONE   *Chapter Thirteen*

Scripture Contemplation: Galatians 6:2

> Bear one another's burdens, and in this way you will fulfill the law of Christ.

Read this verse aloud several times. Where does the Spirit lead you for prayer and action?

FOR REFLECTION

1. What do you notice about Wren's interaction with Mr. Page? How has she been shaped by struggles and losses? How have you been shaped by struggles and losses?

2. Read a modern English translation of "To a Mouse" by Robert Burns. Do you identify with the mouse and the narrator? In what ways?

3. Who are your companions in sorrow and companions in hope? Spend time giving God thanks for them. If no one comes to mind, offer your longings or ache to God.

4. Do you regard sorrow as a negative emotion? Why or why not? How has God met you in your grief? What do you need from God right now?

WEEK THREE: DAY TWO　　　　　*Chapter Fourteen*

Scripture Contemplation: Ecclesiastes 7:21-22

Do not give heed to everything that people say, or you may hear your servant cursing you; your heart knows that many times you have yourself cursed others.

Read the verses aloud a couple of times. Let them lead you into a time of self-examination, confession, and repentance.

FOR REFLECTION

1. When has a first impression of someone impacted your ability to receive them with an open heart? What happened next?

2. When Kit realizes she feels offended by what Bill and Logan said about art, she takes it as a cue to confess her pride and pray God's blessing on them. What causes you to take offense? What helps (or might help) you resist a gravitational pull toward anger and resentment?

3. How prominent are the words *should've, could've, would've* in your vocabulary? Where do those words typically lead your soul? Speak with God about what you notice.

4. How do the words, "Always we begin again" speak to you? How might they speak to your relationships? How do they speak to your first impressions or enduring opinions? What is God's invitation?

WEEK THREE: DAY THREE *Chapter Fourteen*

Scripture Contemplation: Jeremiah 9:23-24

Thus says the LORD: Do not let the wise boast in their wisdom, do not let the mighty boast in their might, do not let the wealthy boast in their wealth; but let those who boast boast in this, that they understand and know me, that I am the LORD; I act with steadfast love, justice, and righteousness in the earth, for in these things I delight, says the LORD.

Slowly read the verses aloud. What do you typically boast (or avoid boasting) about? Which of God's self-descriptions do you most deeply know? How is God seeking to stretch and enlarge your knowledge of who he is and what he delights in? Offer God what you see.

FOR REFLECTION

1. Logan expresses concern about spiritual formation being twisted into a self-improvement exercise, promoting self-discovery and self-fulfillment instead of discipleship and dying to self. How have you seen these dynamics at play in your own life? In your community? How might deeper confidence in God's love for you enlarge your love for God and others? What helps you resist becoming self-absorbed and blind to the well-being of others?

2. Through his questions about diversity at New Hope, Logan holds up a mirror Kit is uncomfortable looking into. What's your reaction to what she sees and how she responds? What helps you keep your heart open when you feel afraid or defensive?

3. How has God led and equipped you as you've navigated difficult, honest conversations about race and justice? Can you identify any fruit from them? If you haven't ever engaged in

these kinds of conversations, would you be willing to? Why or why not? Speak with God about what you see.

4. What does Logan's story about The Talk his African American colleague had with his son open or churn up for you? What do you need from God right now? What do you need from others?

5. What thoughts, emotions, or memories have been stirred for you as you've read Logan and Kit's conversation? What is God's call or invitation? Who could support you as you take a next step?

WEEK THREE: DAY FOUR   *Chapter Fifteen*

Scripture Contemplation: Proverbs 21:2-3

> All deeds are right in the sight of the doer,
>   but the LORD weighs the heart.
> To do righteousness and justice
>   is more acceptable to the LORD than sacrifice.

Read the text slowly. Let the Spirit lead you into a prayerful response.

FOR REFLECTION

1. What catches your attention from Sarah and Kit's conversation? What truth does each of them see? What don't they see or understand? What are you seeing in God's light?

2. What's the difference between "beating yourself up" and responding with confession and repentance when God reveals sin or blindness? Do you regard light as a gift, even when it hurts your eyes? Why or why not?

3. How does Logan define justice? Which aspects of his description of justice challenge you? Convict you? Inspire you? How do you define justice?

4. What does Kit and Wren's conversation about vainglory reveal to you? Do you see evidence of its grip in your own life? Speak with God about what you see, and spend time meditating on his love for you.

5. If you were alongside Kit, how would you pray for her? What do you need prayer for right now?

WEEK THREE: DAY FIVE   *Chapter Fifteen*

Scripture Contemplation: 2 Corinthians 1:8-9

We do not want you to be unaware, brothers and sisters, of the affliction we experienced in Asia; for we were so utterly, unbearably crushed that we despaired of life itself. Indeed, we felt that we had received the sentence of death so that we would rely not on ourselves but on God who raises the dead.

Read the passage aloud several times. Which word or phrase catches your attention and leads you into conversation with God? What is God's invitation to you? How will you respond?

FOR REFLECTION

1. Identify some of Wren's triggered responses, both before and during the retreat session. Are you sympathetic to her? Why or why not?

2. Review Kit's words about faithfully stewarding affliction. When have you attempted to deny or minimize your suffering? How do you respond to the idea that trying to ignore or shrink our pain to a manageable size is a symptom of pride? Speak with God about what you notice.

3. In light of Paul's words to the Corinthians, evaluate the saying "God never gives us more than we can handle." In what ways have you relied on your own strength and resources rather than on the God who raises the dead? Speak with God about what you see and what you need.

4. Ponder some of the words and images Kit uses to describe being "pressed" and overwhelmed by despair. Which ones resonate with you? Why?

5. Like the retreat participants, reflect on times when you have felt crushed and overwhelmed. How have you experienced the

companionship and comfort of Jesus, the bruised and crushed One, in your places of pressing? (If you'd like to pray with Wren's painting, you'll find it in *Remember Me*.) In what ways do you need his companionship and comfort now? Bring what you notice into conversation with God.

WEEK THREE: DAY SIX   *Review*

Return to any questions you were unable to answer this week. Prayerfully review your notes. What pinfeathers are emerging? What seeds are being planted? Talk with God about what you see and what you need.

Group Discussion

Group leaders, read one of the daily Scripture passages a couple of times as your gathering prayer, giving space for silence. Then invite group members to share how the Spirit brought the Word to life.

1. Share something you noticed as you prayed with *Sunflowers* this week.

2. In what ways were you challenged, encouraged, agitated, or inspired by the characters' experiences or interactions? Did God hold up any mirrors for you to see yourselves more clearly? What did you see? How did you respond to what you saw?

3. Share your reactions to Logan and Kit's conversation about diversity and justice. What did their interaction in Kit's office stir in you? How do you define justice?

4. What caught your attention from Kit's retreat session? What are God's invitations to you as you steward affliction and comfort?

5. What does the phrase "Always we begin again" mean to you? How can the group pray for you?

WEEK FOUR

Chapters Sixteen Through Twenty

✦✦✦

VISIO DIVINA: *OLIVE TREES* (1889, NELSON-ATKINS MUSEUM OF ART, KANSAS CITY)

Vincent painted fifteen canvases of olive trees while he was in the asylum at Saint-Rémy, the nearby groves capturing his attention and bringing to mind Christ's suffering in the Garden of Gethsemane (for Wren's reflections about Vincent's olive grove paintings, see *Shades of Light*). Vincent's olive groves inspired her as she painted *Pressed* (see *Remember Me*, "Journey to the Cross").

Let your gaze roam over the painting. What words come to mind to describe the overall mood? What thoughts or feelings are evoked in you as you view it? Now let your eye be drawn to significant details. Which images catch your attention? Why? What do they stir in you? Speak with God about what you notice.

WEEK FOUR: DAY ONE   *Chapter Sixteen*

Scripture Contemplation: Matthew 5:21-24

> You have heard that it was said to those of ancient times, "You shall not murder"; and "whoever murders shall be liable to judgment." But I say to you that if you are angry with a brother or sister, you will be liable to judgment; and if you insult a brother or sister, you will be liable to the council; and if you say, "You fool," you will be liable to the hell of fire. So when

you are offering your gift at the altar, if you remember that
your brother or sister has something against you, leave your gift
there before the altar and go; first be reconciled to your brother
or sister, and then come and offer your gift.

Read Jesus' words slowly and prayerfully. What is the Spirit revealing
to you? How will you respond?

FOR REFLECTION

1. When someone is offended or wounded by something you
   do or say, how do you typically respond? Are you prone to
   dismiss it as an overreaction, or do you seek to listen and
   learn? What helps you humbly and nondefensively engage
   in conversation?

2. How do you react to what Wren overheard Logan say? Does
   this confirm or alter your opinion of him? Why or why not?

3. Think of all the challenges Kit has been trying to navigate, not
   just during the retreat but over the past few months. If you
   were Kit, which ones would you find most stressful? Why?

4. What does Wren's confrontation of Logan stir in you? Why?
   Speak with God about what you notice.

5. If you don't already practice breath prayer, trying using Kit's:
   Inhale: *I can't.* Exhale: *You can, Lord.* What do you need to release

to God right now? What do you long to receive from God? Open your hands as you breathe, releasing and receiving.

WEEK FOUR: DAY TWO   *Chapter Seventeen*

Scripture Contemplation: Psalm 8

O LORD, our Sovereign,
    how majestic is your name in all the earth!
You have set your glory above the heavens.
    Out of the mouths of babes and infants
you have founded a bulwark because of your foes,
    to silence the enemy and the avenger.
When I look at your heavens, the work of your fingers,
    the moon and the stars that you have established;
what are human beings that you are mindful of them,
    mortals that you care for them?
Yet you have made them a little lower than God,
    and crowned them with glory and honor.
You have given them dominion over the works of your hands;
    you have put all things under their feet,
all sheep and oxen,
    and also the beasts of the field,
the birds of the air, and the fish of the sea,
    whatever passes along the paths of the seas.
O LORD, our Sovereign,
    how majestic is your name in all the earth!

Read the psalm aloud a couple of times. Which images or phrases catch your attention and call forth your own praise and prayer? Speak, write, draw, paint, dance, or sing a response of praise and thanks to God.

FOR REFLECTION

1. Which elements in creation reveal God's fingerprints to you? What do you regard as predictable and reliable in a chaotic and broken world?

2. Sarah experiences unexpected emotion when Linda speaks Micah's name. How frequently do you speak the names of loved ones who have died? Are there any memories that remain painful for you? Why? Speak with God about what you see.

3. Do you (like Sarah) have any regrets that you haven't yet offered to God? Anything you did or left undone that continues to haunt you? Anything to ask forgiveness for? Open your hands to release and receive.

4. Meditate again on these words: Love is patient. Love is kind. Who needs an expression of patient and kind love from you? What are you able to offer with God's help?

5. What leads you to wonder and worship? Which regular habits help you to be mindful of the God who is mindful of you?

WEEK FOUR: DAY THREE   *Chapter Eighteen*

Scripture Contemplation: 2 Corinthians 12:7b-10

Therefore, to keep me from being too elated, a thorn was given me in the flesh, a messenger of Satan to torment me, to keep me from being too elated. Three times I appealed to the Lord about this, that it would leave me, but he said to me, "My grace is sufficient for you, for power is made perfect in weakness." So, I will boast all the more gladly of my weaknesses, so that the power of Christ may dwell in me. Therefore I am content with weaknesses, insults, hardships, persecutions, and calamities for the sake of Christ; for whenever I am weak, then I am strong.

Read the text aloud, listening for a word or phrase that catches your attention and invites your prayerful response. What do you need from God today?

FOR REFLECTION

1. Ponder how Kit views "places of pressing." Do any of her descriptions resonate with your own experiences of being pressed? Why or why not?

2. Prayerfully identify the thorns that have tormented you. Which ones have been removed? Which ones have remained? How has the Lord shaped you through them? In what ways has he revealed his grace and glory?

3. What kinds of "what if" questions are most triggering for you? What helps you turn toward God in the midst of agitation? In

what ways have you been driven by fear rather than guided by love?

4. What do you notice about the movement of Kit's soul as she thinks about Logan? Do you identify with her thoughts and feelings? Why or why not?

5. What is God inviting you to see about yourself? Your brothers and sisters in Christ? How will you respond?

WEEK FOUR: DAY FOUR

Chapter Nineteen

Scripture Contemplation: Hebrews 4:12-16

Indeed, the word of God is living and active, sharper than any two-edged sword, piercing until it divides soul from spirit, joints from marrow; it is able to judge the thoughts and intentions of the heart. And before him no creature is hidden, but all are naked and laid bare to the eyes of the one to whom we must render an account.

Since, then, we have a great high priest who has passed through the heavens, Jesus, the Son of God, let us hold fast to our confession. For we do not have a high priest who is unable to sympathize with our weaknesses, but we have one who in every respect has been tested as we are, yet without sin. Let us therefore approach the throne of grace with boldness, so that we may receive mercy and find grace to help in time of need.

Read the first half of the text (vv. 12-13) slowly and prayerfully. What thoughts and emotions rise in you as you picture how the word of God is described? Offer God what you notice.

Now read the second half of the text. Does this change the way you receive the first part? If so, in what ways? Speak with your compassionate high priest about whatever you see and need.

FOR REFLECTION

1. In what ways have the thoughts and intentions of your heart been exposed? Do you try to hide and self-correct, or do you approach the throne of grace without fear? Speak with God about what you need.

2. Prayerfully identify occasions when the thoughts and intentions of your heart have been exposed to others (without your disclosing them). How did you respond? Have there been occasions when you've confessed to others what you've thought or felt about them? What happened next?

3. What catches your attention from Kit and Logan's conversation? What's your definition of a good apology? Is there anyone the Lord is nudging you to move toward in a process of confession and reconciliation? Talk with God about any fears or resistance.

4. If you were Wren or Kit, what would you talk with your counselor or spiritual director about? Why? Now scan your own life. What would you speak with a counselor or spiritual

director about? Is there anything you would avoid speaking about? Why?

5. Are there any areas in your life where you feel stuck and in need of new talking points with God or others? What is God calling you to present as your offering today?

WEEK FOUR: DAY FIVE   *Chapter Twenty*

Scripture Contemplation: Leviticus 19:18

You shall not take vengeance or bear a grudge against any of your people, but you shall love your neighbor as yourself: I am the LORD.

Read the verse aloud several times. What is God revealing to you? Offer your response in prayer.

FOR REFLECTION

1. Spend time looking at Vincent's *The Good Samaritan*. (For additional *visio divina* prayer prompts, see *Shades of Light Study Guide*, p. 35.) What catches your attention? Which character do you resemble or identify with in the story? Speak with God about what the story or painting evokes for you. What do you need and desire?

2. What opportunities have been set before you to "do justice, love mercy, and walk humbly" with your God (Micah 6:8)?

How might God be calling you to steward what has been given to you?

3. What do Kit and Wren disagree about? Whose perspective do you more readily agree with? Why?

4. What makes you angry? How do you express anger? How do you pray it?

5. Is there anyone you regard with contempt or hostility? Which of Kit's or Wren's words speak most directly to you? What is God asking you to do?

WEEK FOUR: DAY SIX   *Review*

Review your responses and notes from the week. Which Scripture readings or questions need more time for reflection and prayer? In what ways have you been provoked, challenged, encouraged, or enlarged this week? Bring it all into conversation with God.

WEEK FOUR

Group Discussion

Before reading an opening Scripture text for silent reflection and prayer, quiet yourselves in God's presence with a breath prayer. Inhale the love of God. Exhale any resistance to God's love. With open hands, release and receive.

1. Which elements in creation reveal God's fingerprints to you? What do you regard as predictable and reliable in a chaotic and broken world?

2. Discuss some of the significant conversations the characters had this week. What caught your attention and why? Did they model anything to you? Expose anything in you? If so, what?

3. In what ways has God used thorns to shape you? Where do you glimpse (or long to glimpse) his power made perfect in your weakness?

4. What makes you angry? How do you express it? Pray it?

5. What has God revealed to you this week as you've prayerfully reflected on your own journey? What next steps are you being called to take? How can the group pray for you?

WEEK FIVE

Chapters Twenty-One Through Twenty-Seven

VISIO DIVINA: *THE BEDROOM* (1888, VAN GOGH MUSEUM, AMSTERDAM)

Vincent painted three versions of his bedroom in the Yellow House in Arles, which was the first home of his own. He described this original rendition in great detail to Theo, saying it was meant "to be suggestive of rest or of sleep in general. In short, looking at the painting should rest the mind, or rather the imagination" (Letter #705, October 1888). Vincent was very fond of this painting and called it one of his best. It became particularly important to him as he was recovering from illness, and he painted the later versions after he was forced to leave his beloved home.

As you ponder the painting, think about your own favorite places of rest and peace. Which curated items bring you joy? How do you best practice resting your mind and imagination? Speak with God about what you see and need.

WEEK FIVE: DAY ONE

Chapters Twenty-One and Twenty-Two

Scripture Contemplation: Psalm 43:1-3

> Vindicate me, O God, and defend my cause
>   against an ungodly people;

from those who are deceitful and unjust
    deliver me!
For you are the God in whom I take refuge;
    why have you cast me off?
Why must I walk about mournfully
    because of the oppression of the enemy?
O send out your light and your truth;
    let them lead me;
let them bring me to your holy hill
    and to your dwelling.

Read the passage aloud a couple of times. Which petitions and declarations best express your own needs and longings right now? Speak them to God for yourself and for others.

FOR REFLECTION

1. How do you define "bearing false witness against a neighbor"? What do you see about your own propensity to jump to conclusions about others? Is there anything God is calling you to confess?

2. How do you approach confrontation? What helps you interpret facts with mercy and respond with grace and truth? What help do you need from God in this?

3. What does Sarah's story about Carol tap in Kit? Do you identify in any way with her internal or external reaction? Offer God anything the scene stirs in you.

4. What does Sarah call her mom to see and name? What has been flushed into the light for you as you journey with the characters? What is God calling you to see and name?

5. Do you have the courage to speak the truth? To name hard things? Why or why not? What does love look like as you move forward in your relationships?

WEEK FIVE: DAY TWO

Chapters Twenty-Three and Twenty-Four

Scripture Contemplation: Psalm 55:4-8

My heart is in anguish within me,
    the terrors of death have fallen upon me.
Fear and trembling come upon me,
    and horror overwhelms me.
And I say, "O that I had wings like a dove!
    I would fly away and be at rest;
truly, I would flee far away;
    I would lodge in the wilderness; *Selah*
I would hurry to find a shelter for myself
    from the raging wind and tempest."

Slowly read the verses aloud a few times. Which images or phrases capture your attention and lead you into conversation with God?

FOR REFLECTION

1. Would you (like Wren) prefer not to know details about the future? Why or why not? If you would prefer to know details,

which ones would you want to know? Why? Speak with God about what you notice.

2. What provisions of manna do you recognize in your own life? What does it mean for you to "daily ingest the mystery" of God's provision? What helps you recognize gifts of grace?

3. What thoughts, emotions, or memories surface as you read about Sarah taking control? What does your response reveal? Offer what you notice to God.

4. Is there anything you (like Kit) feel too tired to argue about? Too weary to resist or conceal? Too worn out to prayerfully explore? Offer your "I can't" to God. What do you need to receive from him?

5. Ponder what Kit sees as she prayerfully explores her resentment and envy. Have you ever refused to speak the truth because of fear? What has that cost you? Talk with God about what you see. What might moving forward in freedom look like?

WEEK FIVE: DAY THREE   *Chapter Twenty-Five*

Scripture Contemplation: Hebrews 13:12-16 (ESV)

So Jesus also suffered outside the gate in order to sanctify the
people through his own blood. Therefore let us go to him
outside the camp and bear the reproach he endured. For here
we have no lasting city, but we seek the city that is to come.
Through him then let us continually offer up a sacrifice of
praise to God, that is, the fruit of lips that acknowledge his
name. Do not neglect to do good and to share what you have,
for such sacrifices are pleasing to God.

Read the verses slowly and prayerfully a couple of times. What
catches your attention? Agitates you? Exhorts you? How is God
calling you to respond? Speak honestly with him about what
you see.

FOR REFLECTION

1. Think about significant perspective shifts you've experienced. Whose story impacted you? What got turned upside
   down? What effect did it have on you? Your loved ones?
   Your decisions?

2. How do you define privilege? In what ways have you experienced abundance? How do you discern how to steward what
   you've received?

3. What opportunities have you had for serving beyond your own benefit or self-interest? What opportunities are before you now? Ask God to reveal them.

4. How would you have handled a confrontation with Carol? Do you feel empathy for Sarah? Why or why not?

5. What kind of movement outside your comfort zone might God be calling you to embrace right now? Speak with him about your willingness or reluctance to be led into something new.

WEEK FIVE: DAY FOUR   *Chapter Twenty-Six*

Scripture Contemplation: Romans 12:14-21

Bless those who persecute you; bless and do not curse them. Rejoice with those who rejoice, weep with those who weep. Live in harmony with one another; do not be haughty, but associate with the lowly; do not claim to be wiser than you are. Do not repay anyone evil for evil, but take thought for what is noble in the sight of all. If it is possible, so far as it depends on you, live peaceably with all. Beloved, never avenge yourselves, but leave room for the wrath of God; for it is written, "Vengeance is mine, I will repay, says the Lord." No, "if your enemies are hungry, feed them; if they are thirsty, give them something to drink; for by doing this you will heap burning coals on their heads." Do not be overcome by evil, but overcome evil with good.

Slowly read the verses aloud. Which instructions catch your attention? Challenge you? Overwhelm you? Inspire you? Have a conversation with God about your response to his Word. Then reframe the passage as prayer: "Lord, let me bless those who persecute me; let me bless and not curse them . . ." As you pray the verses, who comes to mind? Speak with God about what you need.

FOR REFLECTION

1. Which kind of neighborhood would you prefer to live in— Kit's or Mara's? Why? Does anything about Mara's interaction with her neighbors resonate with your own experience or longings?

2. Why does lament sit at the heart of racial justice ministry? How practiced are you in noticing and naming what needs to be grieved, both at a personal and cultural level? How could you more fully embrace the call to "weep with those who weep"?

3. How do you respond to Mara's reservations about Logan and his plans? Do any of her concerns resonate with you? When you think about the work of racial justice, which challenges and concerns would you identify, both personally and in the wider church?

4. Write down everything you've been angry about in the past day/few days. What do you notice? Try keeping an anger journal for the next week. Speak with God about what you see.

5. Identify a next step you feel called to make. Speak with a friend about it.

WEEK FIVE: DAY FIVE   *Chapter Twenty-Seven*

Scripture Contemplation: 1 Thessalonians 5:23-25

May the God of peace himself sanctify you entirely; and may your spirit and soul and body be kept sound and blameless at the coming of our Lord Jesus Christ. The one who calls you is faithful, and he will do this.

Beloved, pray for us.

Slowly read the passage aloud a few times. What catches your attention as you listen and pray? Offer your response to God.

FOR REFLECTION

1. Who are the people who have positively impacted your life? Have you been able to thank them? If you aren't able to thank them, spend time thanking God for them.

2. Who has prayed for you? Who have you prayed for? Which answers to prayer have been most significant for you? Why? Which unfulfilled longings cause your heart to ache? Speak with God about what you see.

3. Explore the movement of Kit's soul during her conversation with Sarah about Carol. In what ways do you identify with her?

4. How have you sought validation for your opinions, struggles, or hurt? Who have you sought it from? Have you received something that satisfied you? Why or why not?

5. Explore the movement of your own soul today. How are you turning toward God? Resisting God? What do you need prayer for? Who can pray with and for you?

WEEK FIVE: DAY SIX   *Review*

What do you notice about the movement of your soul this week? Take some time to prayerfully review your notes. Which Scripture passages caught your attention? Which reflection questions revealed something significant to you? What do you see in your anger journal? Have a conversation with God about whatever has emerged for you.

WEEK FIVE

Group Discussion

Practice *lectio divina* with one of this week's Scripture texts. Share with one another a word or phrase from the text that spoke to you and drew you into conversation with God.

1. Share a gift of grace or provision of manna that you received this week.

2. How did the characters' journeys inspire, frustrate, challenge, or enlighten you? What are God's invitations to you through them?

3. Which reflection questions prompted growth or insight?

4. Share a few things you listed in your anger journal. Are any particular themes emerging for you? How is God meeting you as you offer him your anger?

5. In what ways do you see yourself turning toward God and others? Resisting God and others? How can the group pray for you?

WEEK SIX

Chapters Twenty-Eight Through Thirty

VISIO DIVINA: *PORTRAIT OF PATIENCE ESCALIER*
(1888, PRIVATE COLLECTION)

Vincent painted two portraits of the cowherd and gardener Patience Escalier. (One of the portraits is owned by the Norton Simon Museum in Pasadena, California.) Vincent longed to show the dignity of peasant laborers and to paint people with compassion. In a letter to Theo, he describes his desire to frame Escalier's portrait to hang at the Yellow House (an indication of his fondness for it) and writes, "And in a picture I want to say something comforting as music is comforting. I want to paint men and women with that certain something of the eternal, which the halo used to symbolize and which we seek to confer by the actual radiance and vibration of our colorings" (Letter #673, September 3, 1888).

Let your gaze wander over the portrait. Which details catch your attention or stir your curiosity and compassion? What thoughts, feelings, or memories are tapped as you look at him? What story or wisdom do you imagine Patience might share? What invitations emerge for you? Speak with God about what you see.

WEEK SIX: DAY ONE — *Chapter Twenty-Eight*

Scripture Contemplation: Psalm 19:1-4a

The heavens are telling the glory of God;
　and the firmament proclaims his handiwork.
Day to day pours forth speech,
　and night to night declares knowledge.
There is no speech, nor are there words;
　their voice is not heard;
yet their voice goes out through all the earth,
　and their words to the end of the world.

Read the verses slowly a few times. What testimony does creation speak to you? How do you best listen to creation's voice? Spend time watching and listening today. Offer to God your own testimony about how his glory has been revealed to you.

FOR REFLECTION

1. When have you (like Wren) glimpsed beauty in unexpected places? What kind of beauty do you long to see? Offer God your longings.

2. Which stories have you most frequently shared from your own life? Which ones have the most significance to you? Why?

3. How readily do you demonstrate compassionate curiosity by listening to someone? Whose story needs to be heard and honored? How might you create space to receive their story?

4. What story does your soul need to tell right now? Who might you share this story with?

WEEK SIX: DAY TWO   *Chapter Twenty-Nine*

Scripture Contemplation: Ephesians 4:31–5:2

Put away from you all bitterness and wrath and anger and wrangling and slander, together with all malice, and be kind to one another, tenderhearted, forgiving one another, as God in Christ has forgiven you. Therefore be imitators of God, as beloved children, and live in love, as Christ loved us and gave himself up for us, a fragrant offering and sacrifice to God.

Read the verses aloud a few times. What is God's call to you? How will you respond?

FOR REFLECTION

1. Return to the image of molting. Are there any new losses to navigate or grieve? Any new pinfeathers to notice and name? Any discomfort with the emerging of the new? Speak with God about what you see.

2. How readily do you give others freedom and space to make their own decisions, even if you disagree with them? Are you more inclined to speak or remain silent? How do you discern a wise response?

3. Review the discernment process Kit offers Wren. If you're facing a decision right now, try using this process. What do you notice? Speak with God about what you see.

WEEK SIX: DAY THREE   *Chapter Twenty-Nine*

Scripture Contemplation: 1 John 3:16-18

We know love by this, that he laid down his life for us—and we ought to lay down our lives for one another. How does God's love abide in anyone who has the world's goods and sees a brother or sister in need and yet refuses help?

Little children, let us love, not in word or speech, but in truth and action.

Slowly read the verses aloud a few times. What catches your attention? What is God's call to you? How will you respond?

FOR REFLECTION

1. What does Kit already see? What resonates with you about what she sees and names to Russell? What makes you uncomfortable about what she sees and names? Speak with God about what you see.

2. Do you tend to focus on the needs of individuals or the needs of communities? Why?

3. Identify systems you regard as unjust. How have your views been informed and shaped? What next steps of listening, learning, reflection, prayer, and action is God calling you to take? What kind of input or support could you seek from others as you take a next step?

4. Identify moments of awakening in your own life. How has the Lord led you into deeper insight and vision? When has an awakening led to confession, lament, and repentance?

5. What are you already seeing? How do you feel about what you see? Bring it into conversation with God.

WEEK SIX: DAY FOUR   *Chapter Twenty-Nine*

Scripture Contemplation: Mark 8:22-26

They came to Bethsaida. Some people brought a blind man to him and begged him to touch him. He took the blind man by the hand and led him out of the village; and when he had put saliva on his eyes and laid his hands on him, he asked him, "Can you see anything?" And the man looked up and said, "I can see people, but they look like trees, walking." Then Jesus laid his hands on his eyes again; and he looked intently and his sight was restored, and he saw everything clearly. Then he sent him away to his home, saying, "Do not even go into the village."

Imagine yourself as the blind man and participate in the story with Jesus. What thoughts and feelings arise in you as you interact with him? Have a conversation with God about anything you notice. What do you see?

FOR REFLECTION

1. What opportunities for growth and change do you glimpse in your life? In the midst of clamor and the tyranny of the urgent, what is God calling you to give your attention to right now?

2. How do you typically regard opportunities for growth and change? Speak with God about what you see.

3. Identify some significant liminal spaces or thresholds you've experienced. How has the Lord met you there? What has opened for you on the other side?

4. How do you regard the word *preliminary*? How patient are you with the process of awakening? What words of grace do you need? How might you be reoriented toward hope as you move forward?

5. If you haven't already done so, imagine Jesus asking you, "Can you see anything?" Write or speak your response to him. How does he respond to you?

WEEK SIX: DAY FIVE   *Chapter Thirty*

Scripture Contemplation: Hebrews 12:14-15

Pursue peace with everyone, and the holiness without which no one will see the Lord. See to it that no one fails to obtain the grace of God; that no root of bitterness springs up and causes trouble, and through it many become defiled.

Read the passage aloud several times. Let it shape your conversation with God.

FOR REFLECTION

1. Which kinds of offenses have you found most difficult to forgive? Which ones have you been able to remember without bitterness? Which wounds still need healing? Speak with God about what you see.

2. Have you (like Kit) ever rejoiced in others' wrongdoing? In what ways? How are you being called to pursue, speak, and rejoice in the truth? What does love for others look like right now?

3. Is there anyone you need to seek forgiveness from? What would you name as the truth of your sin? If you haven't already confessed your sin to God, name it to him and receive his grace and forgiveness.

4. Who needs an affirmation of your love right now? Do you feel free to express it? Why or why not?

5. What next steps in the forgiveness and reconciliation journey are you being called to take? What are you afraid of? What do you long for? Offer what you notice to God.

WEEK SIX: DAY SIX   *Review*

Return to any reflection questions you weren't able to respond to this week. (Next week you'll reflect on the second half of chapter thirty.) Prayerfully review your notes. Do any particular themes or invitations stand out to you? Speak with God about what you see.

WEEK SIX

Group Discussion

As an opening exercise, pray with imagination using Mark 8:22-26, or select a Scripture passage from the week to use for *lectio divina*. How is God bringing his Word to life as you listen and respond in prayer?

1. How patient are you with the process of molting or awakening? What evidence of the Spirit's work do you see in your life?

2. Talk about Kit's conversation with Russell. What resonated with you about what she sees and names? What made you feel uncomfortable or defensive?

3. Which reflection questions were most difficult or fruitful for you to process this week? Why?

4. Name some aha moments you experienced during your reflection time. What do you see?

5. What next steps do you believe God is calling you to take? How can the group pray for you?

WEEK SEVEN
Chapters Thirty Through Thirty-Three

✦✦✦

VISIO DIVINA: *SORROWING OLD MAN (AT ETERNITY'S GATE)*
(MAY 1890, KRÖLLER-MÜLLER MUSEUM, OTTERLO)

Known most commonly by the English subtitle Vincent gave the work, *At Eternity's Gate* is based on his earlier lithograph of *Worn Out*. He painted it while he was at the asylum, two months before he died.

Let your gaze wander over the painting. How would you describe the overall mood? Which details catch your attention and call you to linger? Does the title impact the way you read the painting? Why or why not? Speak with God about what you see.

WEEK SEVEN: DAY ONE   *Chapter Thirty*

Scripture Contemplation: Philippians 2:3-8

> Do nothing from selfish ambition or conceit, but in humility regard others as better than yourselves. Let each of you look not to your own interests, but to the interests of others. Let the same mind be in you that was in Christ Jesus,
> > who, though he was in the form of God,
> > > did not regard equality with God
> > > as something to be exploited,
> > but emptied himself,
> > > taking the form of a slave,
> > > being born in human likeness.

And being found in human form,
    he humbled himself
    and became obedient to the point of death—
    even death on a cross.

Read the passage aloud a couple of times. Let the Word lead you in a time of worship, self-examination, repentance, and petition.

FOR REFLECTION

1. If you discovered that your organization, company, or church planned to hire someone who held a position you strongly disagreed with, how would you respond?

2. Have you ever felt as if you've been held hostage by someone else's power play? Have you ever tried to exert power or control in that way? What happened next?

3. Read Logan's post slowly and prayerfully. What resonates with you? Agitates you? Convicts you? Exhorts you? Encourages you? Speak with God about what you see.

4. Ponder Jesus' words, "Do unto others as you would have them do unto you." In what ways is doing good harder than avoiding doing harm? Where are you being called to engage and actively demonstrate costly, incarnational love? Speak with God about what you see.

5. Prayerfully identify the privilege or abundance you have received. How is God calling you to steward what you have been given?

WEEK SEVEN: DAY TWO *Chapter Thirty-One*

Scripture Contemplation: Luke 6:37-38

Do not judge, and you will not be judged; do not condemn, and you will not be condemned. Forgive, and you will be forgiven; give, and it will be given to you. A good measure, pressed down, shaken together, running over, will be put into your lap; for the measure you give will be the measure you get back.

Slowly read Jesus' words aloud. Let them lead you into conversation with God.

FOR REFLECTION

1. What gifts does Chris give Wren in their conversation? Which ones would be most meaningful for you to receive? Why?

2. Identify some "if only" regrets in your life. Which ones still exert power over you? Speak with God about what you see and what you need in moving forward.

3. As Wren listens to Chris's story, she realizes she has a whole new level of forgiveness to address with Casey. In what ways

have you experienced forgiveness as a process rather than an event in your own life? What do you do when you discover more to forgive?

4. Whose side of the story have you neglected to hear? How might you give space and time for listening well?

5. Identify people you have judged. What might you confess to God? To others? Is there an opportunity to move toward someone in repentance and reconciliation? Speak with God about what you see.

WEEK SEVEN: DAY THREE   *Chapter Thirty-Two*

Scripture Contemplation: Matthew 18:21-22

Then Peter came and said to him, "Lord, if another member of the church sins against me, how often should I forgive? As many as seven times?" Jesus said to him, "Not seven times, but, I tell you, seventy-seven times."

Imagine you are Peter, having this conversation with Jesus. How do you hope Jesus will answer your question? How do you respond to his answer? Talk with him about whatever is stirred in you.

FOR REFLECTION

1. Sarah sees that it's easier for her to tick the box of forgiveness without ever being moved by compassion for the offender. In

what ways do you identify with her? Speak with God about what you notice.

2. When have you minimized, denied, or excused someone's sin instead of forgiving it? What does it look like to name sin well?

3. Who provokes you? Why? What is God inviting you to see?

4. Who do you need to forgive again? How does meditating on what Jesus has done for you enable you to forgive the debts of others?

5. Using your imagination to enter the scene, read Jesus' parable of the unforgiving servant (Matthew 18:23-35). Who do you most resemble in the story? What is God's word to you? Have a conversation with God about what you see.

WEEK SEVEN: DAY FOUR   *Chapter Thirty-Two*

Scripture Contemplation: Colossians 3:12-14

As God's chosen ones, holy and beloved, clothe yourselves with compassion, kindness, humility, meekness, and patience. Bear with one another and, if anyone has a complaint against another, forgive each other; just as the Lord has forgiven you, so you also must forgive. Above all, clothe yourselves with love, which binds everything together in perfect harmony.

Slowly read the verses aloud a few times. Which word or phrase comes into bold print for you today? Speak with God about what you hear. What is God's call to you? How do you respond?

FOR REFLECTION

1. How do you practice meditating on and celebrating God's love, mercy, and compassion for you? If this is not a regular spiritual practice, how might such a practice impact your relationship with God, others, and yourself? Speak with God about what you need.

2. Ponder Sarah's reflections and Kit's teaching about forgiveness. What catches your attention? Resonates with you? Challenges you? Provokes you? Speak with God about what you notice.

3. Is there anyone you'd like for God to punish instead of rescue and redeem? Anyone you hold a grudge against? Have a conversation with God about anyone who comes to mind.

4. What next steps is God calling you to take? How might you practice stewarding love and grace?

5. Imagine Jesus asking you, "Do you see anything now?" How do you reply?

WEEK SEVEN: DAY FIVE   *Chapter Thirty-Three*

Scripture Contemplation: Psalm 36:7-9

How precious is your steadfast love, O God!
    All people may take refuge in the shadow of your wings.
They feast on the abundance of your house,
    and you give them drink from the river of your delights.
For with you is the fountain of life;
    in your light we see light.

Slowly read these verses aloud a few times. Which phrases or images catch your attention and stir your longings? Let these lead you into prayer.

FOR REFLECTION

1. What gifts are you most grateful for? Why? Spend time thanking God for them.

2. Have you had experience with people refusing to forgive you? What happened next? Speak with God about anything that remains an open loop for you.

3. Ponder Kit's story about forgiving herself. Is there any invitation for you in it? Offer God what you see.

4. Identify times when light has been disruptive in your life. What has been painful or disorienting for you to see? What has opened up or changed for you as a result?

5. What do you need to release to God today? What do you need to receive from God? Open your hands as a declaration of letting go of control.

WEEK SEVEN: DAY SIX   *Review*

Prayerfully review your responses and notes from the week. (Chapter thirty-three reflections continue next week.) Which Scripture readings or questions need more time for reflection? In what ways have you been challenged and encouraged this week? Have a conversation with God about what you have seen and heard.

WEEK SEVEN

Group Discussion

L eaders, offer one of this week's Scripture texts for *lectio divina*. Share with one another how the Spirit brought the Word to life as you listened and prayed.

1. Jesus says, "Do unto others as you would have them do unto you." In what ways is doing good harder than avoiding doing harm? Where are you being called to engage and actively demonstrate costly, incarnational love?

2. Discuss Logan's blog post. What unsettles you? Resonates with you? Exhorts you? Why?

3. What caught your attention from Kit's teaching about forgiveness? What next steps did you take (or are you being called to take)?

4. Any other insights or reflections to share? How can the group pray for you?

Preparation note for next week: Include a time of feasting as you celebrate what God has done during your journey. (This could be as simple as sharing a plate of cookies around a lit Christ candle.)

WEEK EIGHT

Chapters Thirty-Three Through Thirty-Six

VISIO DIVINA: *FIRST STEPS, AFTER MILLET* (1890, THE METROPOLITAN MUSEUM OF ART, NEW YORK CITY)

During his stay at the asylum, Vincent painted twenty-one copies of work by Millet, an artist who greatly inspired him. Vincent viewed these paintings as "translations" of Millet's original work, as he re-interpreted scenes and figures with colors and brushstrokes. Theo had sent him a black and white photograph of Millet's *First Steps,* which he then rendered in his own style.

Prayerfully scan the painting. What mood does it evoke in you? As you observe the scene, how does it tap your own memories, longings, sorrows, or joys? Where do you find yourself in the painting? Which details catch your attention? How does this painting speak to your life with God and others? Have a conversation with God about any insights and invitations that emerge.

WEEK EIGHT: DAY ONE   *Chapter Thirty-Three*

Scripture Contemplation: Proverbs 31:8-9

> Speak out for those who cannot speak,
>   for the rights of all the destitute.
> Speak out, judge righteously,
>   defend the rights of the poor and needy.

Slowly read the verses aloud. What might God be calling you to speak up about? Who might God be calling you to advocate for? How might you use your resources on behalf of others? Talk with God about any resistance, fear, or desire.

FOR REFLECTION

1. Do you tend to shy away from controversy or welcome it? Which experiences have shaped how you approach potentially divisive issues? Talk with God about your response.

2. What does it mean to pursue racial justice and righteousness, both for you personally and in the body of Christ? What do you need from others and from God in this journey? What is your prayer?

3. Where are you being invited to step forward into more freedom? Into more patient love for others? Into giving up control? How might you practice these things?

4. What have you begun to see more clearly? What does a faithful response look like? What is your next yes?

5. What do you hope the Lord will do in you, for you, and through you as you offer your next yes?

WEEK EIGHT: DAY TWO　　　*Chapter Thirty-Four*

Scripture Contemplation: Romans 15:1-7

We who are strong ought to put up with the failings of the weak, and not to please ourselves. Each of us must please our neighbor for the good purpose of building up the neighbor. For Christ did not please himself; but, as it is written, "The insults of those who insult you have fallen on me." For whatever was written in former days was written for our instruction, so that by steadfastness and by the encouragement of the scriptures we might have hope. May the God of steadfastness and encouragement grant you to live in harmony with one another, in accordance with Christ Jesus, so that together you may with one voice glorify the God and Father of our Lord Jesus Christ.

Welcome one another, therefore, just as Christ has welcomed you, for the glory of God.

Slowly read the passage aloud. What challenges you? Exhorts you? Let the Word lead you into a prayerful response.

FOR REFLECTION

1. Think about your experiences of being welcomed. Which memories are most significant to you? Why?

2. How have you been shaped by seasons of waiting? In what ways are you currently waiting for God to act on your behalf? On behalf of others? Speak with God about any impatience, frustration, or lack of hope.

3. Which details catch your attention from Mara's church? Do any of them stir your longings, inspire you, or make you uncomfortable? If so, why? Offer what you notice to God.

4. What do you notice about the way Mara navigates the confrontation between Brooke and Wren? What do you notice about Wren's posture with Brooke? Do either of them model anything for you? If so, what?

5. What's your own style of navigating conflict? When have you been frustrated by lack of progress? When have you been encouraged by a good resolution? Speak with God about any broken relationships you're still waiting to see healed, and give God thanks for those that have been reconciled.

WEEK EIGHT: DAY THREE   *Chapter Thirty-Five*

Scripture Contemplation: 1 Peter 4:8-10

Above all, maintain constant love for one another, for love covers a multitude of sins. Be hospitable to one another without complaining. Like good stewards of the manifold grace of God, serve one another with whatever gift each of you has received.

Slowly read the passage aloud a couple of times. Which word or phrase catches your attention and calls you into deeper reflection? Have a conversation with God about what you see and need. What is God's call to you?

FOR REFLECTION

1. Are you able to receive words of encouragement, or do you tend to focus on your failures and regrets? What good words do you need to spend time savoring?

2. Read Barb's note to Kit. Then prayerfully ponder opportunities you've had for stewarding affliction. What comfort, compassion, or encouragement have you received? What comfort, compassion, or encouragement have you been able to offer others?

3. Which weaknesses are you reluctant to boast about? In which weaknesses have you glimpsed God's power being made perfect? How might boasting about your weaknesses be an encouragement to others? Speak with God about what you see.

4. After Wren shares her story with Mr. Page, he offers affirmation about how she has used her gifts. What opportunities have you had (or do you currently have) for stewarding your gifts? Whose affirmation has been life-giving to you? What kind of affirmation do you desire?

5. Spend time praying Katherine's words: "For all I've done well, thank you for your grace. For all I've done poorly, thank you for your grace." How might you practice celebrating God's grace in your life? Who might celebrate with you?

WEEK EIGHT: DAY FOUR *Chapter Thirty-Six*

Scripture Contemplation: Psalm 126:5-6

> May those who sow in tears
>   reap with shouts of joy.
> Those who go out weeping,
>   bearing the seed for sowing,
> shall come home with shouts of joy,
>   carrying their sheaves.

Slowly read the verses aloud, letting them guide you into conversation with God. Spend time praying for those who sow in tears and who wait to reap with joy.

FOR REFLECTION

1. Prayerfully examine an online image of Vincent's *The Siesta* (1890, Musée d'Orsay, Paris). What catches your attention or stirs your longings? How do you practice rest, both individually and with others? What is God's invitation to you?

2. Do you have any favorite hymns or choruses? Which lyrics have meant the most to you? Why? Spend time praying with them. (If you're meeting with a group, print out a verse to share.)

3. What memories are most precious to you? Spend time giving God thanks for the people, places, and experiences that have been gifts of love to you.

4. What gifts of love might you offer others? Who needs words of encouragement, affirmation, or thanks? Ask God to guide your thoughts, inspire your creativity, and enable you to follow through with concrete action.

WEEK EIGHT: DAY FIVE　　　　　　*Chapter Thirty-Six*

Scripture Contemplation: Galatians 6:7-10

Do not be deceived; God is not mocked, for you reap whatever you sow. If you sow to your own flesh, you will reap corruption from the flesh; but if you sow to the Spirit, you will reap eternal life from the Spirit. So let us not grow weary in doing what is right, for we will reap at harvest time, if we do not give up. So then, whenever we have an opportunity, let us work for the good of all, and especially for those of the family of faith.

Read these verses aloud a few times. How does the image of sowing and reaping speak to you? What is God's call to you? Offer your response in prayer.

FOR REFLECTION

1. Slowly read Hannah's words of encouragement to Kit. Which words speak most deeply to you? Which tap your longings? What do you need to take to heart? Talk with God about what you notice.

2. What do you hope happens next for the characters? At New Hope? How do these longings mirror longings for your own life?

3. How does the image of molting speak to you now? What feathers of hope do you perceive in your own life? Speak with God about what you see.

4. Where have you sown seeds? What evidence of a harvest do you see—or hope to see? What are you still waiting for God to do? How might you celebrate what God has already done?

5. What's your next yes? Offer it to God and speak it to a friend who can support and encourage you as you move forward.

WEEK EIGHT: DAY SIX   *Review*

Prayerfully review your notes from the study. In what ways has the Lord met you as you've walked with him? Offer God your gratitude and longings.

WEEK EIGHT
Group Discussion

eaders, light the Christ candle and use one of this week's Scripture texts to open your time in prayer. Invite members to read a verse from a favorite hymn or chorus. Share food as you discuss the reflection questions.

1. What caught your attention from the characters' journeys this week? Share any aha moments with one another.

2. What do you hope happens next for the characters? At New Hope? How do these longings mirror longings for your own life?

3. How does the image of molting speak to you now? What feathers of hope do you perceive in your own life?

4. What feathers of hope do you perceive in one another's lives? Take time to offer affirmation about each member's growth and gifts. Practice receiving and taking to heart this encouragement from each other.

5. Share your next yes. What next steps might you take as a group? How can you pray for one another?

6. Close your time in prayer by reading the blessing from Numbers 6:24-26 in unison: "The LORD bless you and keep you; the LORD make his face to shine upon you, and be gracious to you; the LORD lift up his countenance upon you, and give you peace."

Lightning Source UK Ltd.
Milton Keynes UK
UKHW010711080522
402532UK00001B/30